Mrs. Jeepers'
Scariest
Halloween Ever

Want more Bailey School Kids?
Check these out!

#1–50

SUPER SPECIALS

#1–7

#1–10

And don't miss the . . .

HOLIDAY SPECIALS

Swamp Monsters Don't Chase Wild Turkeys
Aliens Don't Carve Jack-o'-lanterns
Mrs. Claus Doesn't Climb Telephone Poles
Leprechauns Don't Play Fetch
Ogres Don't Hunt Easter Eggs

Mrs. Jeepers' Scariest Halloween Ever

by Debbie Dadey
and
Marcia Thornton Jones

illustrated by John Steven Gurney

A
LITTLE APPLE
PAPERBACK

SCHOLASTIC INC.
New York   Toronto   London   Auckland   Sydney
Mexico City   New Delhi   Hong Kong   Buenos Aires

*To the love of my life, Eric.
Thanks for sharing both the good and the
scary times.
—DD*

*To Jared and Lisa:
May your future be free from vampires, were-
wolves, and basement monsters that go Squeeeeak.
Thump. Squeeeeak. Thump.
—MTJ*

Activity illustrations by Heather Saunders.

ISBN 0-439-77527-2

12 11 10 9 8 7 6 5 4 3 2   5 6 7 8 9 10/0
                                           40
Printed in the U.S.A.
First Scholastic printing, August 2005

Contents

1

Halloween Fun?

"Psssst!" Eddie tried to get his best friend Howie's attention during class time.

Howie looked over at Mrs. Jeepers. Their teacher was across the room helping a girl named Issy with her math assignment.

Some third-graders thought Mrs. Jeepers was a vampire. After all, she came from Transylvania and lived in the old Clancy Estate. Only a vampire would dare live in a creepy place like that. Most kids were scared of Mrs. Jeepers. But Eddie was not most kids.

When Howie was sure Mrs. Jeepers wasn't looking, he glanced over his shoulder at Eddie. "Leave me alone! We have to do our math," Howie whispered.

The entire third-grade class was making designs out of square-shaped and triangular pattern blocks. Howie had already figured out how to make a bird and a house. Melody, another good friend, had made a cat and dog.

Math was the last thing Eddie wanted to do. After all, it was October twenty-fifth, less than a week before one of his favorite holidays. He wanted to have a bit of Halloween fun!

Eddie waited until his friend Liza, who sat in front of him, had her head bent over her math puzzle. Liza shoved a strand of blond hair behind her ear before turning a triangle upside down and pushing it against a square. She was concentrating hard. That's when Eddie struck. He reached in his desk and pulled out a long piece of wire. At the end of the wire was a very big, very hairy spider. It wasn't real, but Liza wouldn't know that.

The pretend spider wiggled and squirmed on the end of the wire as Eddie carefully moved it across the floor. Then, ever so slowly, he guided the spider toward Liza's leg.

Up and up the spider went. It crawled over Liza's ankle. It squirmed past her knee. It wiggled toward her lap. Eddie had to bite his lip to keep from laughing out loud as the spider made its way to Liza's arm.

That's when Liza saw something out of the corner of her eye. She did what any normal kid would do.

"ARRRRRRRRGH!"

Liza's scream brought the entire class to a stop. She jumped up from her seat and swatted at the spider. "Get it off me! Get it off me!" she yelled.

Mrs. Jeepers appeared next to Eddie's desk. Her eyes flashed and her hand flew to the green brooch at her throat. Whenever Mrs. Jeepers rubbed that brooch, magic seemed to happen.

The green stone in her pin glowed. Light bounced off of it, and it grew brighter.

3

All of a sudden, the wire felt hot in Eddie's hand. "Ouch!" he hollered. He dropped the wire as if the spider had bitten his thumb. It landed on the floor with a click.

Mrs. Jeepers took a step toward Eddie. There was absolutely nowhere for him to run. Eddie was trapped!

2

Trapped

Eddie scooted backward so far that he fell out of his seat. Mrs. Jeepers seemed to grow taller as she towered over him.

"I have had enough," Mrs. Jeepers said in her Transylvanian accent. Slowly, her green fingernails reached toward Eddie. "Give me your toy."

Eddie shook his head. "It's mine," he said.

Nobody talked back to Mrs. Jeepers. Ever. Liza nearly fainted. Howie closed his eyes. Melody gulped. A few other kids gasped.

Mrs. Jeepers' eyes flashed. Her fingers danced across her brooch. On the floor, the fake spider twitched. It wiggled. Then it jumped straight up into Mrs. Jeepers' hand.

"Thank you," Mrs. Jeepers said as she turned and carried the spider back to her desk. "I'll hold on to this for now. Please continue your math."

"But . . . but . . . I *need* that spider," Eddie stammered. "Can I have it back? Please?"

Eddie only said please when it was important. Like now.

Mrs. Jeepers slowly turned. "Toy spiders are never *needed*," she said.

"This one is," Eddie said bravely. He wasn't backing down.

The third grade at Bailey School was always quiet. That's the way Mrs. Jeepers liked it. But even on the best days, there was the sound of feet tapping on the floor, pencils scratching against papers, and kids sniffling. Suddenly, all those sounds were gone. Everyone sat frozen, watching Mrs. Jeepers and Eddie. It was so quiet you could have heard a napping ghost snore.

"Why would a boy like you need a

spider like this?" Mrs. Jeepers asked, holding the spider up. It danced on the end of the wire just two inches in front of Eddie's nose.

Eddie stood up next to his desk. He cleared his throat and spoke in his bravest voice. "Because I am going to win the Halloween costume contest, and it's part of my costume," he said.

"No, you're not," Melody blurted. The words slipped out before she could stop them.

Issy gasped. A girl named Carey dropped her book. A kid named Huey thumped his head down on his desk and covered his eyes. Melody slapped her hand over her mouth to stop herself from saying anything else.

Mrs. Jeepers flashed her eyes in Melody's direction. "Contest?" she asked. "What contest?"

Eddie knew more than anyone about the contest. He'd been planning his costume all year long. "Every year, the city

9

has a big Halloween festival at the mall," he said.

"Kids can trick-or-treat," Howie said quietly.

"They have games," Liza added. "Like the cakewalk."

"Cakewalk?" Mrs. Jeepers repeated. "How do cakes walk?"

A few kids giggled, but they fell silent when Mrs. Jeepers' green eyes turned in their direction.

"The cakes don't walk," Liza answered politely. "It's a game like musical chairs, and the winners get cakes."

"But the best prize of all is for the costume contest," Eddie said. "This year, the prize is a computer game of the winner's choice, and I'm going to win it. I know just what game to get — *Ghoul School.* That way I can play every night."

"Not if *I* win the contest," Melody snapped.

Mrs. Jeepers silenced both of them with a glance. "So it is a contest for a game that you feel is, shall we say, worth your time and effort," she said.

Eddie nodded. "My grandmother wouldn't buy me the game, but *everyone* else has it."

"I don't," Melody reminded him. "Not yet, anyway. But I will when I win the contest."

Liza didn't like the way Mrs. Jeepers listened to Eddie and Melody. Usually, their teacher didn't allow arguing.

Eddie rolled his eyes at Melody. "You don't stand a chance. Besides, I *need* it. Ben has *Ghoul School* and I'm tired of hearing him brag about how good he is at it. I have to get it so I can beat the pants off him."

Ben was a fourth-grader at their school. Everyone knew that Ben and Eddie didn't get along.

Mrs. Jeepers tapped her fingers on her green brooch again. Then she smiled her odd little half smile. When most teachers smiled, it was a good thing, but when

Mrs. Jeepers smiled, it sent shivers up the spines of every kid in the room. That's because her extra-pointy eyeteeth glistened.

"This contest," she said. "What kind of costumes are required?"

Eddie puffed out his chest. "Scary is best. I'm going to be a giant spider with eight hairy legs. That's why I need that spider back. I'm hanging little spiders all over a sweatshirt as part of my costume."

"That's a dumb costume," Melody said. "Not everyone likes scary."

Mrs. Jeepers turned to her, and Melody hunkered down in her seat. "What is your costume?" Mrs. Jeepers asked.

Melody sat up a little straighter. "I wanted to keep it a secret," she said. But when Mrs. Jeepers' green fingernails reached for her brooch, Melody added, "But I'll tell you. I'm going to dress as an Olympic gold-medal winner."

"No," Mrs. Jeepers said simply.

"No?" Melody and Eddie said together.

"No," Mrs. Jeepers repeated. Her pointy-toed boots click-clacked to the front of the room. She turned and faced the class. "For this Halloween contest," she announced, "you will all complete a report and dress as your favorite book character, or a figure from history."

Liza clapped her hands. "That means my costume is perfect," she said. Melody gasped, and Howie groaned. In fact, most of the kids didn't look happy at all.

"No way," Eddie blurted. "I'm not turning Halloween into a school project."

Mrs. Jeepers faced Eddie. "You will," she said. "Or else . . ."

3

Hog-tied

"I thought for sure you were vampire bait," Liza told Eddie.

It was Halloween night. The sun was sinking in the sky, and a cool breeze rattled through the bare tree limbs.

Howie nodded. "It's a good thing you changed your mind about your costume and followed Mrs. Jeepers' directions." Eddie had ditched his spider costume and dressed as a Viking.

Eddie whacked at a bush with his pretend club. A cold wind blew by, and dried leaves flew through the air. The four friends were in their costumes, trick-or-treating on their way to the mall for the Bailey City Halloween Bash. Eddie had been sure he would win the mall contest until Mrs. Jeepers had made the whole thing into a homework assignment. He had spent the rest of the week trying to think of a costume that was scary enough to win the contest but would still make his teacher happy. It hadn't been easy. Thinking was not Eddie's favorite thing to do.

"This is all your fault," Eddie snapped at Melody. "If you had just kept your mouth shut, I could've worn my giant spider costume."

"It never would have won," Melody said. "Everyone would've picked my Olympic gold-medal winner over your silly spider costume any day."

"Mrs. Jeepers should have sent you to the principal's office," Liza said. She was still mad at Eddie for scaring her with the toy spider. "You deserved to get in trouble." She reached out and flicked the helmet off Eddie's head.

Eddie dived after his helmet before it

crashed to the ground. "Aw, lighten up," Eddie said. "It was just a teensy-weensy spider. It wasn't real!"

"Forget the spider," Melody suggested, shoving her ray gun between them. She had spent the last two days wrapping cardboard boxes in foil so her costume would look like the robot from her favorite science fiction book.

Liza straightened the Statue of Liberty crown on her head. "I will, as soon as Eddie the Rotten apologizes."

"I'm not apologizing to you or to anyone else," Eddie snapped.

Faster than they could say "Howdy Doody," Howie reached over and dropped his cowboy lasso around Eddie. Then Howie pulled it tight. Eddie's bag of candy slipped from his hands and he couldn't move.

"Hey! What are you doing?" Eddie yelped.

"I'm hog-tying you until you stop fighting with Liza," Howie said.

"Let me go, before you make us late for the costume contest that I plan to win!" Eddie ordered.

"You're not going to win," Melody said. "*I'm* going to win."

"Nuh-uh," Liza said. "Everyone is going to love my Statue of Liberty costume. It's *very* patriotic. Not like your silly robot, Melody."

"We're not going anywhere until you all stop fighting," Howie drawled in his best cowboy voice. "After all, winning a contest isn't as important as your friends."

Eddie rolled his eyes at Liza. Liza glared at Eddie. Melody frowned at Liza. Howie looked at them all.

"Fine," Eddie said. "I'm sorry. Now let me go!"

Howie waited for Liza and Melody.

"All right," Liza said finally. "I'm sorry."

"Me, too," Melody added.

Howie grinned. "That's more like it!"

Eddie shrugged off the lasso and picked

up his bag of candy. "You better not have ruined my costume," he warned Howie.

Melody pointed her ray gun down a side street. "It's faster if we turn down Delaware Boulevard," she said.

"Are you sure it's safe?" Liza asked. Her voice sounded small in the growing darkness. "After all, the Clancy Estate is that way."

The four friends peered down the street. The sun had dropped behind the trees, and shadows stretched like dark fingers in their direction. The four friends could barely make out the hulking shadows of the old mansion down the block.

Every kid in Bailey City knew about the Clancy Estate. It had been empty for decades and everyone believed it was haunted. Things got even worse when Mrs. Jeepers moved to town and decided to live in the old house.

"We'll walk on the other side of the street," Melody said.

"Mrs. Jeepers can't get us," Eddie argued. "We're not in school."

"I don't think vampires have to follow school rules," Liza said.

Howie patted Liza on the shoulder. "It will be okay," he said. "As long as we all stick together."

They slowly made their way down Delaware Boulevard, with Howie in the lead. The Clancy Estate loomed before them. Its rusty iron fence reached around the yard like an evil black snake. The bare limbs of a tree reminded Liza of a skeleton's long fingers. When a loose shutter thumped against the side of the house, Melody dropped her fake ray gun.

The four friends hid in the shadows across the street and peered up at the Clancy Estate. They all remembered the time they had seen movers carrying a long wooden box into the basement of the old house. The box looked suspiciously like a coffin.

"I can't believe our teacher *lives* there," Eddie said.

"Only a vampire would want to sleep in a place like that," Liza said. Her voice trembled more than a little when she spoke.

The branches on a nearby bush shook and something rustled through a patch of weeds.

"Quick, let's get out of here before Mrs. Jeepers or one of her batty friends sees us!" Melody hissed.

But as they turned to go, a huge shape jumped out of the shadows and blocked their way.

4

Mummy

"Ben!" Melody yelled. "What are you doing?"

Ben had a reputation for being a professional troublemaker. Since he was in the fourth grade, he liked picking on third-graders. Especially Eddie. Ben grinned from behind the rags of his mummy costume. "Scaring you silly, that's what I'm doing," he bragged.

"You couldn't scare me if you tried," Eddie snapped, raising his Viking club high in the air.

"What's that?" Ben asked with a snort. "A baseball bat?" Then he looked at Melody, Liza, and Howie, and laughed at their costumes. "You all look like something out of a textbook," he said.

"Keep your mouth shut, or I'll use your

toilet-paper costume to keep it shut for you," Eddie threatened.

"I'm so scared," Ben said. "See me shake?"

"We had to dress like this," Howie explained. "Our teacher made us."

Ben laughed even louder. "There's no way you'll win the mall contest dressed like that," he said. "It looks like Eddie will never get his chance to beat me at *Ghoul School*."

"You want to bet?" Eddie argued.

"Hold it right there," Liza said, stepping between Eddie and Ben. "We'd better get to the mall before the costume contest begins, or *none* of us will have a chance."

Ben grinned again. "None of you do, anyway," he said, "because I'm going to win that contest."

Eddie shook his club in the air and yelled, "I'm going to win! My costume is ten times better than yours. In fact, I'm better than you in everything."

"Eddie!" Liza gasped. "That's not nice."

"It's also not true," Ben said, shoving the mummy rags off his mouth. "I know for a fact that I'm braver than you."

"Are not," Eddie said, pushing his nose up to Ben's face.

Ben stared Eddie straight in the eyes and said, "Am too."

"Come on, guys," Howie said. "Let's get to the mall." Howie put one leg over his stick pony and got ready to gallop off to the contest.

"The mall can wait," Ben said. "I know

how to prove that I'm braver than Eddie. That is, if he isn't too chicken to even try it."

Melody tugged on Eddie's arm. "Whatever it is," she whispered, "don't do it."

Eddie pulled his arm away from Melody. "I'm not chicken, and I'll prove it."

"Then you won't be afraid to go trick-or-treating at the Clancy Estate," Ben said with a snicker.

When Liza gasped, her Statue of Liberty crown slid down over one eye. Howie was so surprised, he dropped his stick horse. Melody tripped over it and fell to the ground.

"No!" Liza squealed at Eddie. "You can't go over to Mrs. Jeepers' house. It's not s-s-safe."

"What's wrong?" Ben teased. "Are you scared of your own teacher?"

"Yes," Liza admitted, "especially when it's almost dark and it's the spookiest night of the year."

But Eddie couldn't stand for someone

to think he was scared of anything. Especially if that someone was Ben. "I'll do it," Eddie said, accepting the challenge.

"Are you crazy?" Melody cried.

"We can't let him go alone," Howie told Melody and Liza.

"Oh, yes, we can," Melody said. "If Eddie is nutty enough to go up to a haunted house on Halloween, then he deserves whatever he gets."

"I don't need you or anybody else to come with me," Eddie said. He glared at Melody, then looked both ways and crossed Delaware Boulevard. Eddie had his hand on the rusty iron gate in front of the Clancy Estate when Howie called out, "Wait for me!"

Howie left the girls with Ben and walked across the street. Liza looked at Melody and sighed. "Come on," Liza said, helping Melody up. "I know we're going to regret this, but let's go."

27

5

Death Grip

The gate creaked as Eddie pulled it open. "I should give Mrs. Jeepers a can of oil for Christmas," he muttered.

"A can of paint would be good, too," Liza said, joking so she wouldn't feel so scared. She looked up at the huge mansion as the four kids walked up the crumbling sidewalk toward the front door. In the moonlight, Liza noticed paint peeling off the house, and a broken shutter hanging by one hinge. But what really gave her the creeps were the huge bats flying around the attic window.

Melody looked back at Ben. He smiled and waved from the other side of the street. Liza grabbed Eddie's hand and Melody held Howie's. The four kids took a deep

breath and stepped onto the wooden porch. The rotting boards creaked with every step they took. Liza squeezed Eddie's hand harder and harder.

"Ouch!" Eddie complained. "You're about to break my fingers."

"Oh, sorry," Liza whispered. She loosened her death grip on Eddie's hand just a little.

"Did you hear that?" Melody asked, stopping in the middle of the porch.

"It's just the wind," Howie said.

The kids listened. Sure enough, the wind moaned and groaned through the dead tree beside the old mansion.

"Okay," Eddie said bravely. "Let's do this." He tucked his Viking club under his arm and reached out to knock on the door.

"Wait!" Liza cried. "I'll give you all my Halloween candy if you turn around and walk away right now."

Eddie looked at Liza in disbelief. "You would give me all your candy?"

Liza nodded. She was so scared, her Statue of Liberty crown shook. "Let's get out of here before one of those bats turns us into vampires."

Eddie looked up at the full moon. Three bats flew in and out of a broken attic window. It wasn't the attic that had Eddie worried, though. It was the horrible sound he heard coming from the basement.

Squeeeeeeak. Thump. Squeeeeeeak. Thump. "M-m-maybe it's that coffin opening up," Liza said, backing away from the front door.

The noise got louder and louder and louder. *Squeeeeeeak. Thump. Squeeeeeeak. Thump.*

"Run!" Howie shouted.

6

Like Bugs in a Web

Howie raced down the steps and jumped over a fat tree root that poked through a crack in the sidewalk.

Melody and Eddie ran after him, but Liza tripped on the crooked steps and stumbled to the ground. Her feet got all tangled in her long Statue of Liberty gown.

Squeeeeeeak. Thump. Squeeeeeeak. Thump. The noise was just on the other side of the heavy wooden door.

"Help me," Liza whimpered. She could not untangle her feet, so she crawled down the sidewalk.

Melody grabbed Howie and Eddie just before they reached the curb. The three friends skidded to a halt. "Wait! Liza's in trouble," Melody told them.

"Good grief," Eddie mumbled. But he dug in his heels and darted back up the sidewalk. Howie and Melody followed right behind him.

When they reached Liza, Eddie bent down and grabbed one of her elbows. Melody held the other. Howie picked up Liza's feet.

Squeeeeeeak. Thump. Squeeeeeeak. Thump. SQUEEEAAAAK!

"Holy Toledo!" Eddie yelled.

"We'll never escape in time!" Liza cried.

"Never say never," Melody said. "Let's get out of here."

Eddie, Melody, and Howie half-carried and half-dragged Liza across the dead grass in the front yard. Just as they reached the corner of the house, they heard the front door swing open. With a giant push, Eddie, Melody, and Howie heaved Liza behind a tangled thicket of bushes on the edge of the Clancy Estate.

"Shh," Eddie warned as they all ducked down behind the bushes.

The four friends held their breaths.

Thump. Thump. Thump.

Something very very big made its way to the edge of the porch. Then there was total silence.

"It's waiting," Eddie whispered. "For us."

"We'll never get out of here," Liza moaned. "We're trapped, like bugs in a spider's web."

"Speaking of webs," Melody said with a tremor in her voice. "S-s-something's crawling on my leg!" She slapped at her ankle.

"Whatever you do, don't make a sound," Howie warned, grabbing Melody's hand.

"We can't stay here forever," Eddie said. "We'll miss the costume contest. If I don't win *Ghoul School*, Ben will never let me hear the end of it."

"This is more important than a video game," Melody told him. "Besides, your costume would never beat mine."

"Shh," Howie hissed. "Fighting isn't

going to save us from whatever is on that porch."

"Neither will hiding," Eddie said. "We have to escape — now."

"But we can't go through the front gate," Liza whispered. "We'd be seen."

"We'll crawl to the backyard," Eddie told his friends. "Then we'll climb the fence and be home free." Eddie used his Viking club to push the tangled bushes aside. Slowly, he crawled forward on his belly, staying as low to the ground as possible. His three friends followed.

No kid had *ever* willingly gone into the backyard of the old Clancy Estate, but that's right where Eddie was headed.

A shutter slapped against the wall near the back door, making Liza jump. "I don't like this," Liza said.

"Don't worry," Melody said. "It's just the wind."

Liza pointed a shaking finger. "It's not the wind I'm worried about. It's *them*."

A cloud moved from in front of the

moon. Moonlight shone over the yard for a brief moment, and they could all see where Liza pointed.

From the lawn, statues stared at them with empty eyes. Not just one or two statues, but dozens. There were big ones and little ones. There were statues of people, and even ones that looked like animals. They all seemed to be glaring right at the four kids.

"They're only lawn sculptures," Eddie said matter-of-factly.

"Those don't look like normal statues," Melody said.

Howie nodded. "They look like the kind that are in cemeteries," he added.

"Why would our teacher have cemetery statues all over her backyard?" Liza asked.

"I don't know," Melody said, "and I don't want to find out. Let's go through a neighbor's yard and get out of here before someone catches us."

"We can't," Howie pointed out. "The fence is higher back here."

It was true. The iron fence surrounding the backyard was at least six feet tall. Even if they could climb that high, they wouldn't dare. The huge spikes on top of the fence made it impossible to get over.

"I have an idea," Eddie said, grabbing the rope that went with Howie's cowboy costume. Before Howie could say "Hi-Ho, Silver," Eddie had knotted one end of the rope. Then he slung the rope over the branch of a tree and pulled until the knot caught and held firm. Using the rope for support, Eddie walked up the side of the giant tree trunk. Once he had reached the place where the tree trunk split into two giant branches, he dropped the rope back down to his friends.

Liza went next, with Melody giving her a push from behind. Then Melody and Howie made their way up the tree. Before long, all four of them were clinging to tree branches. "Now what?" Liza asked.

Eddie pointed at the long, fat tree branch that reached over the high fence and into the neighbor's yard. "We crawl along that branch. When we get to the end, we jump to the ground."

Liza looked down at the ground. It seemed very, very far away. "I can't jump that far!" she said.

"Then you can face whatever is in that window," Eddie said calmly, pointing back at the Clancy Estate.

Liza, Melody, and Howie looked at their teacher's old house. Climbing the tree had put them at eye level with one of the windows. What they saw inside made Liza gasp out loud.

7

Close Call

Someone stood inside the mansion with their back to the window. It wasn't Mrs. Jeepers. They knew that for a fact, because whoever it was had two heads.

Back in the tree, the four friends planned their escape. "The way I see it, you have three choices," Eddie said. "One, you can sit up here and wait for one of those heads to turn around and see you. Two, you can go back to the front yard and try sneaking past whatever is on the porch. Or three, you can follow me."

"Lead the way," Liza said. "And make it fast!"

Eddie shinnied to the end of the branch. As he moved, the branch bent lower and lower until it rested on top of the fence.

When he got to the end, Eddie tied Howie's rope around the end of the branch and then hopped down into the neighbor's yard. He pulled hard on the branch to keep it from slinging his friends off as they made their way to freedom.

Finally, all four of them stood on the other side of the fence.

"This way," Eddie said as he raced to the curb, slowing down just long enough to make sure there were no cars coming.

Liza's and Melody's sneakers pounded the pavement beside Howie.

"Where have you guys been?" Ben asked when they reached him. "I was getting ready to go win that contest without you."

"Quick," Eddie whispered in the dark. "Behind the trees."

Melody and Liza huddled with Eddie in the shadows. Howie grabbed Ben and pulled the fourth-grader out of sight.

Liza leaned over to catch her breath. Her heart was pounding so loudly, she was sure the two-headed monster in Mrs. Jeepers' house could hear. Melody held her side, where she had a cramp from running.

Whatever had stepped out on the front porch was still there. "What is it?" Howie whispered.

Ben pulled his arm away from Howie's grasp. "It's just Mrs. . . ."

He didn't get a chance to finish. Eddie slapped a hand over Ben's mouth, cutting him short.

A cloud passed over the moon, turning the night sky as black as a bat's wing. Liza squinted her eyes and tried to see through the darkness. "I think I s-s-see s-s-something," she stammered.

Ben pulled loose from Eddie's hand. "I told you," Ben hissed. "It's just your teacher."

Liza shook her head. "Mrs. Jeepers' eyes don't glow like that," she said. "Her eyes are green."

The kids followed Liza's gaze. Sure enough, two eyes the color of a pumpkin pierced the night, staring straight in their direction.

Liza and Melody ducked down to the ground. Howie and Eddie hugged the tree trunk. Ben hunkered down behind a bush.

 As the cloud moved on across the sky, and moonlight shone through the night, the

kids heard the front door of the Clancy Estate slam shut.

Howie took off his cowboy hat and wiped his forehead with his bandanna. "Whew," he said. "That was a close call."

"Nothing even happened!" Ben argued. "You guys wimped out. You ran from your teacher!"

"That wasn't our teacher," Liza said. "It couldn't be."

"We saw something," Melody added. "Something big. Very big."

"The only big thing around here is you," Ben interrupted. "You're a BIG bunch of cowards."

"Are not," Eddie snapped.

"Are too," Ben said, jabbing Eddie in the chest with his finger.

Howie stepped between the two boys. "This is silly," he said. "We're missing all the Halloween fun over a fight that no one can win."

"You're right," Eddie said with a grin.

"Ben can't win this fight because *he's* the chicken. And chickens never win fights."

"I'm no coward," Ben argued. "After all, *you're* the ones that ran. Not me."

"That's because you were too chicken to even go!" Eddie said.

"I'm not afraid, and I'll prove it," Ben said.

"Great," Eddie said. "March over there, knock on the door, and find out who — or what — has those orange eyes."

"No problem," Ben said. "You wait here. I'll be back."

Without another word, Ben checked for traffic and stomped across the street. A loose piece of toilet paper from his mummy costume fluttered behind him.

He glanced over his shoulder to make sure Melody, Howie, Liza, and Eddie were watching. They were.

"Shouldn't we tell him about the two-headed monster?" Liza asked.

Eddie shook his head. "He'd never believe us."

Ben pounded on the door.

Squeeeeeeak. Thump. Squeeeeeeak. Thump.

Ben backed away from the door and waited for someone to answer it.

"Run. Run. Run," Liza whispered.

But Ben didn't run.

The door to the Clancy Estate opened and then, right before their eyes, Ben was swallowed up by Mrs. Jeepers' haunted house.

8

The Princess and the Pirate

"Something's wrong," Liza said. "Very wrong."

"No kid in his right mind would go inside the Clancy Estate," Melody said.

"We did, once," Eddie reminded them. Melody tried to forget about the time they had sneaked into the basement of their teacher's house to see what was in that long wooden box. The basement had been dark, and the long wooden box had been locked. From the inside.

"No kid in their right mind would go in there *alone*," Howie added.

"Ben has never been in his right mind," Eddie said.

A bat swooped past a nearby street-light, and a dog howled a few streets away.

Wind whispered through the branches as the kids waited. They waited and waited, but Ben didn't reappear.

"What if he never comes out?" Liza asked.

"Then good riddance, if you ask me," Eddie said. He picked up his bag of candy and headed in the direction of the mall. "I have candy to collect and a costume contest to win. I'm out of here. I don't have any more time to waste on Ben or anybody else."

Liza grabbed his bag of candy to stop him. "We have to save Ben!"

"No, we don't," Eddie said, trying to pull his treat bag loose from Liza's grip.

"She's right," Howie said.

"What're you going to do?" Eddie asked. "Knock on the door and step on the monster's big toe until it lets Ben go?"

Melody, Howie, and Liza stared at Eddie. They hated to admit it, but Eddie had a good point. There was no way they could fight a two-headed monster, a vampire teacher, and whatever had those big orange eyes.

"See?" Eddie said. "We can't do anything, so we might as well go get some chocolate. Chocolate solves everything."

"We can't leave Ben in there alone," Melody said.

The kids were still arguing over whether to stay or go when two girls turned down Delaware Boulevard.

"Great," Eddie said. "It's Carey and Issy. This Halloween has just gone from bad to worse."

Carey and Issy were both in their class at school. It was a known fact that Carey took turns either hating Eddie or liking Eddie. *Really* liking him.

Carey spotted the kids as she came down the street. She stopped and batted her eyelashes at Eddie. She was dressed as a princess from her favorite fairy tale. Carey held out her dress and twirled around. "Do you like my costume?" she asked Eddie.

"*Squawk*! Pretty dress. Pretty dress," said the parrot on Issy's shoulder.

Issy was dressed as a pirate. She dressed as a pirate every Halloween so she could take Filbert, her pet parrot, trick-or-treating. She liked to take Filbert with her everywhere.

"Aren't you going to the mall?" Issy asked. "I hear they're having a bake sale. I want to get a pie for my grandmother."

"Pumpkin pie. *Squawk*! Pumpkin pie," said Filbert.

"We can't go," Liza said.

"Why not?" Carey asked.

"Because," Melody started to explain. "Mrs. Jeepers . . ."

". . . is giving out great big chocolate bars," Eddie blurted before Melody could finish.

"*Squawk*! Chocolate bars. Chocolate bars," Issy's parrot repeated.

"Really?" Issy and Carey said together.

Melody, Liza, and Howie stared at Eddie as if he'd just turned into a real Viking.

"That's right," Eddie said before his friends could stop him. "Huge candy bars. Ben's in there right now. You really should go and get some before you go to the mall. I'm sure they won't last long, because Ben will eat them all before he leaves. Maybe you can get him out of there. We tried, but he wouldn't listen to us. You know Ben. He never listens to me."

"Will you wait for us?" Carey asked, batting her long eyelashes at Eddie. "Then we can walk to the mall together."

"You go inside and get Ben, and then we'll all go to the mall," Eddie said.

"Okay. Let's go," Issy said.

"Go. Go. *Squawk!*" Filbert added.

"Don't leave without me," Carey told Eddie. Then she turned and followed Issy across the street.

Liza watched the princess and the pirate make their way up the crooked steps to the Clancy Estate. "You shouldn't have lied, Eddie," she said.

"You wanted to save Ben, right?" Eddie asked. "Well, sometimes you have to break a few rules to help someone."

"Shh," Melody warned. "The door is opening."

Sure enough, the hinges creaked and the door slowly opened. Issy and Carey looked up at whoever was inside the door. And then, as if in a trance, the two girls stepped slowly through the open door and disappeared inside the Clancy Estate.

"No!" Melody called into the darkness.

Issy's parrot's voice shattered the stillness on Delaware Boulevard. "No! No!" he said. "*Squawk!*"

The door closed. And there was total silence.

9

Viking Spies

"Oh, no!" Liza cried. "The Clancy Estate is eating up kids!"

Melody gulped. "We have to do something."

"We can't just knock on the door," Howie said. "We'll disappear, too. No one will ever know what happened to us."

Liza shuddered. "Hundreds of years from now, it will still be a mystery."

"I know what we can do," Eddie said, holding his Viking club high in the air. "We'll investigate. We'll be spies." Eddie loved pretending to be a spy. Secretly, he wanted to be an FBI agent when he grew up, or a famous athlete.

Melody shook her head. "I'm pretty sure Vikings weren't spies."

"Are you kidding?" Eddie said. "Vikings were the first investigators. Didn't you know that they probably discovered America long before Christopher Columbus was even born?"

Melody looked at Eddie in surprise. "I knew that," she said, "but I didn't think you were listening when Mrs. Jeepers told us about Vikings."

Eddie nodded. "I listen when it's interesting, but don't tell Mrs. Jeepers that."

"Come on," Howie said. "Let's hurry, before something terrible happens to Issy, Carey, and Ben."

Nobody said a word as they crossed the street. All of them were afraid that something awful had already happened to their friends. A sudden banging noise rang through the air, and Eddie jumped behind a dead tree. Howie, Liza, and Melody squeezed in behind him.

"Are we going up to the porch?" Liza whispered.

"No," Eddie told her. "Mrs. Jeepers might hear us coming. Let's go around to the back again."

The mansion loomed above them as the kids tiptoed around the corner. When another bang echoed through the night, Liza leaped up on Melody's back. "What is that?" Liza whimpered.

"I don't know," Melody said. "But you need to calm down. We can't help anyone if you're a basket case."

Liza took a deep breath and hopped off Melody's back. Liza didn't calm down, though. Her heart raced. She had cold chills up and down her back. Sweat trickled down her face from under her Statue of Liberty crown. When she heard the banging noise again, she screamed.

Howie slapped his hand over her mouth, and Eddie pointed to the back of the mansion.

"Look," he whispered. "That's what is making the banging noise."

The full moon revealed that the basement door of the Clancy Estate had been left open. Every time the wind blew, the old door banged shut and popped open again.

"Come on," Eddie said, starting down the steep, dark basement steps.

"Where are you going?" Melody asked.

"You guys wanted to find Ben. So let's go," Eddie said. Then he disappeared into the blackness.

10

Mrs. Jeepers and Friends?

"Why is the door open?" Liza whispered.

Melody shrugged. "Mrs. Jeepers must have forgotten to lock it."

"That's dangerous. Anyone could just walk into her house," Liza said.

Howie took off his cowboy hat and scratched his head. "I guess when you're a vampire, you don't have to worry about burglars. If they come in your house, you just bite their necks."

Melody giggled nervously. "Why don't we go home and call the police?" she suggested.

"The police would take too long," Howie said. "We have to follow Eddie."

"Following Eddie is never a good idea," Melody told Liza and Howie.

Suddenly, Eddie popped his head up out of the dark staircase. Liza was so startled, she fell on her behind! "Come on," Eddie snapped. "Let's go. I still have a contest to win."

Liza didn't want to, but she also didn't want to be left alone in the dark. She followed her friends. She held her breath as the kids stepped into the damp basement.

"Phe-ew," Melody whispered. "This place still stinks. You'd think Mrs. Jeepers would clean it up."

"She's too busy giving us homework," Eddie complained.

Liza reached into her treat bag and pulled out a small flashlight. She shone it around her teacher's basement. Broken chairs and cardboard boxes filled the cavelike room.

"That's where the coffin is," Melody said, pointing to a shadowy corner.

"Are you sure it's a coffin?" Liza asked. "After all, why would a teacher have a coffin in her basement?"

Howie shrugged. "It could be where she naps, but it's probably just an ordinary box that she stores stuff in."

Eddie shook his head. "No, it's a coffin. Look, I'll show you." Eddie twisted and turned past a stack of boxes, then stopped dead still.

"What's wrong?" Melody asked, heading through the boxes toward Eddie.

"You're never going to believe this," Eddie said. "The box is gone. It vanished." Sure enough, when Liza shone her flashlight into the corner, the kids could see the outline of a huge box on the dusty floor, but the box was nowhere to be seen.

"What happened to it?" Melody asked.

"Maybe whoever was in the coffin is walking around upstairs," Eddie said slowly.

Just then, the single lightbulb dangling from the ceiling switched on. The four kids dived behind a pile of boxes. Liza dug her fingernails into Eddie's arm as footsteps slowly thudded down the steps.

It wasn't just one pair of footsteps, either. There were lots and lots of footsteps.

"Let's get out of here," Melody hissed. Eddie made a mad dash for the outside door, but unfortunately, so did Liza, Howie, and Melody. The kids tripped over one another and fell to the floor in a pile.

Tears filled Liza's eyes. "We're dead monster mush," she moaned. She looked up to see who the footsteps belonged to. It was their teacher, Mrs. Jeepers.

She wasn't alone.

There was a two-headed monster and a creature with orange eyes floating over

its head. There was even a zombie with a vulture perched on its shoulder. In fact, a crowd of drooling, bloody monsters stood right behind their teacher.

Mrs. Jeepers slowly grinned. Her eyeteeth glistened. Liza looked around desperately to find a place to run or hide.

The monsters stepped closer and closer and closer, and there was absolutely no way out!

11

Trouble

Melody closed her eyes. Liza buried her head in her costume's sleeve. Howie's cowboy hat fell over his face. But Eddie stood up and waved his Viking club in the air.

"All right, you dumb monsters!" Eddie yelled. "Bring it on. I'm ready for you!"

Liza lifted her head and whimpered, "Eddie, don't go asking for trouble."

"It's too late for that," Melody said, opening her eyes. "Trouble already found us."

"Eddie's right. We have to save ourselves!" Howie shouted, lifting his stick horse in the air. Melody held up her pretend space gun, and Liza pointed her torch at the monsters. The four kids backed up to a pile of boxes, holding their weapons in front of them.

The monsters came closer and closer. Finally, Mrs. Jeepers started laughing.

"What's so funny?" Eddie asked, waving his club to keep the monsters away.

Then all the monsters laughed. They laughed so hard, one of them fell on the basement floor and rolled around. Another had tears running down his face from laughing so much.

The vulture flapped its wings. "*Squawk!* So funny, so funny," it said. It sounded very much like Filbert the parrot.

Liza stomped her foot. "It's not polite to laugh at your victims before you eat them."

That just made the monsters laugh harder. "Don't you recognize us?" one of the monsters asked before batting her eyes at Eddie.

Eddie leaned closer to the monsters and peered at their faces. One of the monsters was a mummy, sort of like Ben had been before. Only this mummy was much more real-looking. "Carey? Ben? Issy? Is that you?" Eddie asked.

Three monsters giggled. Another monster said, "You should have seen the looks on your faces."

"Huey!" Howie growled, recognizing a voice from school. "What are *you* doing here?"

"We're all here getting cool costumes for the contest," Huey said, waving his arm at the other kid monsters. "Mrs. Jeepers has trunks of stuff from scary books."

"I bet she does," Melody said softly.

"Why did you frighten us?" Liza said. "That wasn't very nice."

Mrs. Jeepers put her hand to her brooch. "I must apologize. But you should remember that it is not polite to sneak into a person's home, even if it is Halloween."

Liza's face turned red under the bare lightbulb. "Um, we're sorry about that."

"We only did it because we didn't know

what happened to Ben, Carey, and Issy," Eddie explained.

The Carey monster put her hand on Eddie's arm. "You mean, you were worried about little old me?"

Eddie jerked his arm away and nodded toward Liza and Melody. "*They* were worried."

"Worried. Worried," Filbert repeated with a flap of his vulture wings.

Mrs. Jeepers cleared her throat. "If we are going to be in the contest, we should leave now."

"Let's go!" the Ben monster shouted. Mrs. Jeepers and the monsters turned to clomp up the stairs. Mrs. Jeepers closed the outside door as she walked by.

"Let's get going," Eddie said to his friends.

"Wait just a minute," Liza whispered. "How can we be sure those monsters are really kids?"

Howie shrugged. "It sure sounded like them."

Liza shivered in the damp basement. "What if they're trying to trick us into *thinking* they're kids? Maybe those aren't costumes after all. Maybe, just maybe, those monsters are the real thing. What if our friends have been turned into monsters . . . forever?"

Melody took a deep breath. "There's only one way to find out."

Eddie nodded toward the steps. "Let's go."

12

Runaway Pumpkin

Liza gulped and followed her friends up the steps. The four kids found themselves in a large hallway. A huge cobweb-covered chandelier hung from the high ceiling. A massive wooden staircase curved down to meet the dusty bloodred carpet under their feet.

Howie sneezed at the musty smell in the air. "I guess Mrs. Jeepers has the cobwebs there as Halloween decorations."

Melody shook her head and softly said, "Those aren't decorations. They're real." She pointed to a small skeleton hanging halfway up the stairs.

"That looks real, too," Eddie said. "I bet it's some third-grader who wouldn't behave." Eddie was joking, but the four kids got very quiet after that. When Mrs.

74

Jeepers led the parade of monsters out the front door, the friends gladly followed, happy to escape the Clancy Estate alive.

The monsters followed Mrs. Jeepers down Delaware Boulevard. They walked slowly, as if they were caught in a bad dream. When the kids turned left onto Main Street, Liza grabbed Melody's arm.

"What if Mrs. Jeepers and her monsters plan to turn the Halloween contest into a monster picnic?" Liza asked. "*We* could be the main course!"

"Don't worry," Melody said. "Those are just costumes."

"How can you be sure?" Liza argued. "Something about the way they move doesn't seem right."

Howie nodded. "She has a point," he said. "Most kids would be laughing and running. They're definitely not acting normal."

Howie, Melody, Liza, and Eddie followed the monster parade in silence until they got to the mall. "I have an idea,"

Eddie said. "All we have to do is get them to act normal. Then we'll know they're not monsters."

"How do we get monsters to act normal?" Howie asked.

"Leave that to me," Eddie said. "I have a plan."

As soon as the kids were inside the mall, Eddie ran up to the Carey monster and pulled her hair.

"EEEEKKK!" Carey screeched. "What did you do that for?"

"Just checking to make sure you're real," Eddie said with a grin.

"How's this for real?" Carey asked. She kicked Eddie in the shin as hard as she could.

"Ouch!" Eddie yelled, as he fell backward into a huge Halloween decoration. A giant pumpkin the size of a minivan fell over and rolled down the center of the mall.

"Look out!" Liza squealed. "Runaway pumpkin!"

Howie tried to stop the pumpkin, but it knocked him to the ground. In fact, many adults tried to halt the huge rolling ball, too. They all got thrown to the side. Costumed kids shrieked and dived out of the way as the pumpkin rolled toward them.

"It's a pumpkin-tastrophe!" Melody shouted.

The screams and shouts all died down when Mrs. Jeepers' finger gently rubbed her green brooch. Suddenly, the pumpkin came to a dead stop in front of a large podium in the center of the mall. At the podium stood the mayor, the main judge of the costume contest.

"Uh-oh," Eddie said. "I'll never win now. The mayor thinks I caused that pumpkin mess."

"You did," Liza told him as she helped Howie up from the floor.

"That's not the point," Eddie said. "Besides, this contest is rigged. Mr. Cooper is helping to judge! He doesn't like me. He's always warning me to be quiet."

Mr. Cooper was a librarian at the Bailey City library. He held a clipboard and stood on the podium next to the mayor. Every costumed kid tried to get close to the two judges.

"Mr. Cooper is going to like Mrs. Jeepers' monster costumes," Liza said. "They're all from famous books."

"Books, shmooks," Eddie grumbled. "Vikings were an important part of our history. Our country might not even be

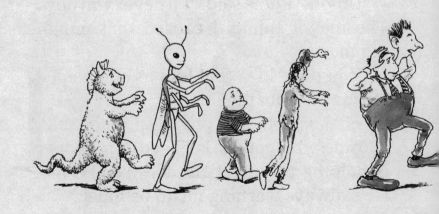

here if it wasn't for the Vikings. I should win this contest."

Liza stood up straight. "What about the Statue of Liberty?" she asked. "Lady Liberty stands for the light of freedom in our country."

"Cowboys helped build the west," Howie pointed out, defending his costume.

Melody shrugged. "My costume is the future. We'll all be living in space by the time we're adults, especially if we

81

don't stop polluting our environment. I should win."

Just then, spooky organ music echoed throughout the mall. Mrs. Jeepers and her monsters slowly marched toward the mayor.

"Winning won't matter once Mrs. Jeepers and her monsters invade Bailey City," Liza whispered. "Look!"

Stomp. Stomp. Stomp. Monster feet moved in time to the music, slowly following Mrs. Jeepers. The monsters stepped closer and closer to the mayor. A few held out their arms like zombies. Several of them groaned. The monster with the orange eyes wiggling on wires over her head moaned. The two-headed monster held both heads as if he had a headache. Filbert squawked and flapped his wings as the monsters formed a line in front of the mayor.

Stomp. Stomp. Stomp. They marched like they were in a trance. In the center of them all stood Mrs. Jeepers, smiling her odd little half smile.

"Mrs. Jeepers used her magic brooch to turn them all into monsters," Liza whimpered.

"Keep toward the back," Melody said, "in case we have to make a quick getaway."

"This is it," Liza gasped. "Mrs. Jeepers is taking over Bailey City. It's the end of life as we know it!"

13

The Winners

Suddenly, the mayor held up his hands and the music stopped. Mrs. Jeepers and her troop of monsters grew silent.

"Thank you for coming out and joining in the Halloween fun," the mayor said. "Mr. Cooper and I had a tough time deciding on a winner. Let's give all of our young contestants a big hand!"

"Get on with it," Eddie mumbled as the crowd clapped politely. "Tell us who won already."

"Shh," Liza hissed under her breath. "Get ready to run."

Eddie didn't want to run. He wanted to win. A pyramid of computer games was stacked up on the podium. *Ghoul School* was at the very top. Eddie's fingers itched. He couldn't wait to get his hands on that game.

"I am truly amazed by all of the costumes here," the mayor went on. "I must admit, however, that Mrs. Jeepers and her group of Bailey School students were inspiring with their realistic costumes from books."

"That's because monsters are her specialty," Eddie grumbled.

"Shh," Melody warned him.

"There were so many excellent costumes," the mayor continued, "that the Bailey City library has graciously agreed to help sponsor not just one prize but *two* prizes this year."

At that, the whole audience cheered. "Now we can both win," Melody told Eddie. For the moment, she forgot the monsters lined up by Mrs. Jeepers.

Eddie had his fingers crossed behind his back as the mayor said, "And the first winner is . . ."

"Let it be me . . . please let it be me," Melody whispered.

". . . Kilmer Hauntly!" the mayor announced.

"Kilmer Hauntly?" Eddie snapped. "Who is that?"

"He's the new kid in fourth grade," Howie said.

The crowd clapped as a tall, square-headed kid dressed as Frankenstein's monster accepted his prize from Mr.

Cooper. "That isn't even a very real-looking costume," Eddie complained.

"Listen," Howie said. "There's one more winner."

"It's got to be me," Eddie said.

"No," Melody said, elbowing Eddie in the side. "Me."

"And the second winner is . . ." the mayor began.

Melody and Eddie both held their breath.

"Mrs. Jeepers and her monster troop!" the mayor shouted.

"What?" Eddie yelled. "That's not fair!"

No one heard Eddie, because they were all cheering for the group of monsters as Mrs. Jeepers stepped forward to accept their prize from Mr. Cooper.

Eddie sank to the floor when Mrs. Jeepers passed up the *Ghoul School* computer game and pointed to *Math Facts for Fun* instead. Eddie held his head in his hands and stared at the dirty mall floor until two pointy-toed boots clacked under his nose. He looked up and up and up from the floor. Mrs. Jeepers stood in front of him. She smiled, making sure Eddie could see her pointy eyeteeth.

"Thank you for telling me about the costume contest," his teacher said in her strange Transylvanian accent. "Now you can work on your math facts every single day. Because of you, all the boys and girls in our classroom will be able to practice math."

Eddie groaned, and Mrs. Jeepers disappeared out the door into the night. He groaned again when monsters surrounded him.

Carey and Issy took off their masks. So did most of the others. Without their monster masks and makeup, it was plain to see that they were the same old kids from school.

Carey smiled at Eddie. "Better luck next year, Eddie-poo," Carey said. She giggled and batted her eyelashes.

"Eddie-poo! Eddie-poo!" squawked Filbert.

"I knew you wouldn't win," Ben teased. "Just like you'll never win a game of *Ghoul School*. At least, not as long as I'm around."

"I guess they weren't monsters after all," Liza admitted as Ben turned to congratulate Kilmer. "This was the scariest Halloween ever, but it was silly for me to think kids could be monsters."

Melody reached out to stop Eddie from tripping Ben with his Viking club. "Silly, except for one kid," she said. "And that's Eddie. Bailey City's BIGGEST monster . . . ever!"

Haunted Puzzles
and
Spooky Activities

Haunted House Maze

See if you can
make your way
out of the
spooky
Clancy Estate!

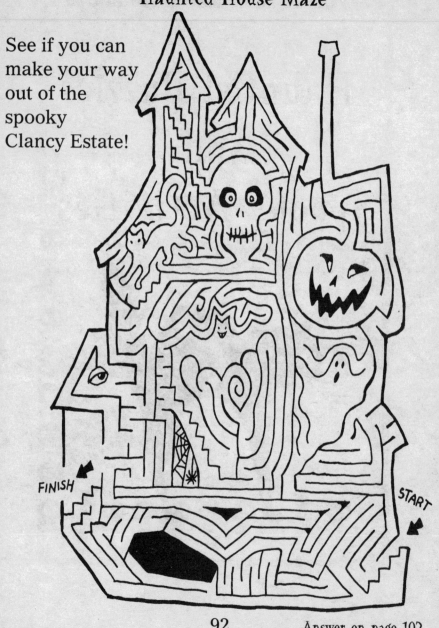

FINISH

START

Answer on page 102

Weird and Wacky Word Search

Find the words hidden in the skeletons below. Words can be horizontal, vertical, diagonal, and even backward.

Words: VAMPIRE, VIKING, BATS,
COSTUME, SPIDER, MUMMY, COWBOY,
WEB, CANDY, CARVE, MASK

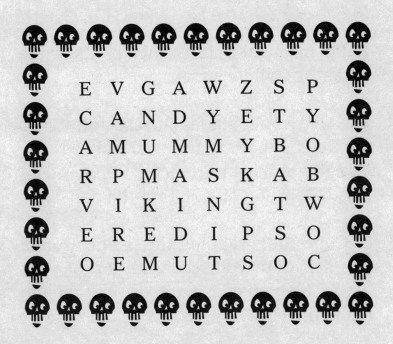

```
E V G A W Z S P
C A N D Y E T Y
A M U M M Y B O
R P M A S K A B
V I K I N G T W
E R E D I P S O
O E M U T S O C
```

Answer on page 102

Make your Own Mummy Costume!

You will need: several rolls of toilet paper, clear or white tape, white clothing and shoes

1. Put on a white shirt, white pants, white socks, and white shoes.

2. Start at your ankles and carefully wrap the toilet paper around your entire body. You might need a friend or family member to help so you don't rip the paper.

3. Continue wrapping the paper around yourself until you reach the top of your head. If the paper tears, use the tape to mend the rips.

4. Tape the ends of each toilet paper strand to another strand so you don't unravel.

5. Make sure you leave space for your eyes, nose, and mouth.

6. Instead of toilet paper, you can also use white surgical bandages, or long torn strips of an old white sheet.

BONUS FUN!

Use red food coloring as fake blood to make your mummy costume even scarier!

Find the Differences!
Can you find ten differences between these two pictures?

Answer on page 103

On pages 100–101 you will find a passage taken from *Mrs. Jeepers' Scariest Halloween Ever*. But, uh-oh—some words are missing! Can you help the Bailey School Kids fill in the blanks?

Before you even look at the passages, fill in the blanks below. Try to pick words that are as silly, funny, or spooky as possible. When you are done, copy the words in order into the story. And get ready to laugh out loud! You'll have your own brand-new BSK adventure!

Your name: _____

Noun: _____

Plural noun: _____

Name of a teacher: _____

Noun: _____

Color: _____

Body part: _____

Animal: _____

Verb ending in –ing: _____

Adjective: _____

Same name of a teacher: _____

Different body part: _____

Your name: _____

Verb: _____

Plural noun: _____

Verb: _____

Tears filled (_____)'s
                  Your name

eyes. "We're dead monster (_____),"
                              noun

she moaned. She looked up to see

who belonged to the (_____).
                        plural noun

It was their teacher, (_____).
                         Name of teacher

She wasn't alone.

"There   was   a   two-headed

(_____).   A   monster   with
     noun

(_____) eyes floating over its
    color

(_____). There was even
      body part

a zombie with a (_____)
                            animal

perched on its shoulder. In fact, a crowd

of (_____), (_____)

verb ending in –ing   adjective

monsters surrounded their teacher.

(_____) slowly grinned.

Same name of teacher

Her (_____) glistened.

Different body part

(_____) looked desperately

Your name

around to find a place to (_____)

verb

or hide.

The (_____) stepped closer

plural noun

and closer and closer, and there was

absolutely nowhere to (_____)!

verb

Puzzle Answers

Haunted House Maze
(page 92)

Weird and Wacky Word Search
(page 93)

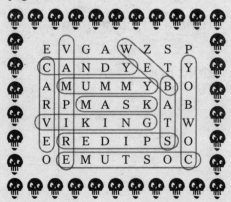

Find the Differences
(pages 96-97)

About the Authors

Debbie Dadey and Marcia Thornton Jones have fun writing stories together. When they both worked at an elementary school in Lexington, Kentucky, Debbie was the school librarian and Marcia was a teacher. During their lunch break in the school cafeteria, they came up with the idea of the Bailey School Kids.

A few years ago, Debbie and her family moved to Fort Collins, Colorado. Marcia and her husband still live in Kentucky, where she continues to teach. How do these authors write together? They talk on the phone and use computers and fax machines!

Learn more about Debbie and Marcia at their Web site, www.BaileyKids.com!